Grandfather
Twilight

Grandfather Twilight

Barbara Berger

Philomel Books

NEW YORK

Published by Philomel Books,
a division of The Putnam & Grosset Group,
200 Madison Avenue, New York, NY 10016.
Published simultaneously in Canada. All rights reserved.
Sandcastle Books and the Sandcastle logo are trademarks
belonging to the Putnam & Grosset Group
Printed in Hong Kong by South China Printing Co. (1988) Limited.

Library of Congress Cataloging in Publication Data
Berger, Barbara,   Grandfather Twilight.
Summary: At the day's end, Grandfather Twilight
walks in the forest to perform his evening task,
bringing the miracle of night to the world.
[1. Twilight—Fiction. 2. Night—Fiction] I. Title.
PZ7.B4513Gr 1984   [Fic]   83-19490
ISBN 0-399-20996-4(hc)
15 14
ISBN 0-399-21596-4(pbk)
11 13 15 14 12

To Dad

Grandfather Twilight lives among the trees.

When day is done, he closes his book,
combs his beard, and puts on his jacket.

Next, he opens a wooden chest that is
filled with an endless strand of pearls.
He lifts the strand, takes one pearl from it,
and closes the chest again.

Then, holding the pearl in his hand,
Grandfather Twilight goes for a walk.

The pearl grows larger with every step.

Leaves begin to whisper. Little birds hush.

Gently, he gives the pearl to the silence
above the sea.

Then Grandfather Twilight

goes home again.

He gets ready for bed.

And he goes to sleep.

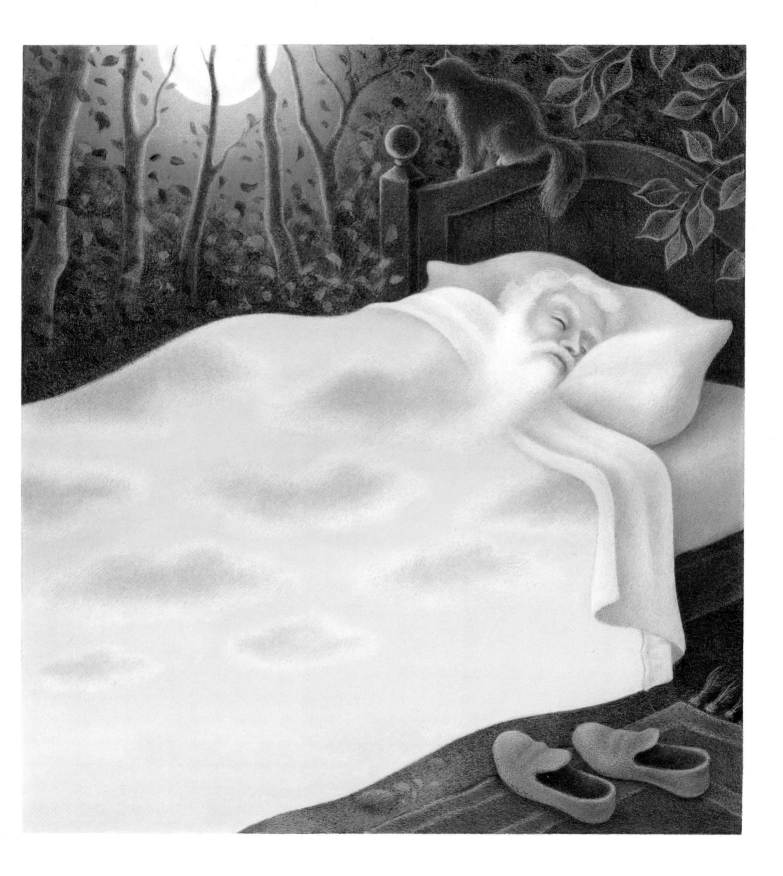

Good night.